THE SUPERTEAMS

ENGLAND

THREE LIONS ACTION FROM 1998/99

mustard

First published in 1999 by Mustard

Mustard is an imprint of Parragon

Parragon
Queen Street House
4 Queen Street
Bath BA1 1HE, UK
Copyright ©Parragon 1999

British Library Cataloguing-in Publication Data.

A catalogue record for this book is available from the British Library.

ISBN 1 84164 246 0

Printed in Italy

CONTENTS

England's Year

It was a strange 12 months for England. **Glenn Hoddle** took England to **France 98**, but his diary of the tournament damaged him and further problems away from the pitch eventually cost him his job. **Howard Wilkinson** turned to some old faces, before new players were then brought in by **Kevin Keegan**. There were plenty of changes of formation, too.

DEFENCE

England's number one keeper, **David Seaman**, did not have his best year, but **Nigel Martyn** established himself as second choice. In front of them, **Sol Campbell, Tony Adams, Gary Neville, Graeme Le Saux** and **Gareth Southgate** played in the World Cup. **Martin Keown, Phil Neville, Rio Ferdinand** and **Michael Gray** also played.

MIDFIELD

David Batty, Paul Ince, David **Beckham, Darren Anderton** and **Paul Scholes** were the main midfielders in France, with **Rob Lee, Paul Merson** and **Steve McManaman. Jamie Redknapp** came back from injury to feature late, along with **Nicky Butt. Tim Sherwood** and **Lee Hendrie** both made debuts.

Wembley, home of England

TURNSTILES
◄ ABC
DEF

TURNSTILES
GHJ ►
KLM

IN THE HOT SEAT

ATTACK

Captain **Alan Shearer** had many partners, thanks in part to injuries to France 98 star **Michael Owen**: notably **Teddy Sheringham**, **Andy Cole**, and **Robbie Fowler**. **Kevin Phillips**, **Ian Wright**, **Dion Dublin** all featured, too, though mainly in friendlies.

Glenn Hoddle became player-manager with Swindon then Chelsea after a fine career on the pitch with Spurs. He became England coach in 1996. **Howard Wilkinson** won the 1992 League title with Leeds and was working for the FA when he briefly took charge of the national side. **Kevin Keegan** found fame with Liverpool, then Hamburg, Southampton and Newcastle United.

Thrills And Spills

England's World Cup campaign got off to a **good start** against **Tunisia**, as Alan Shearer and Paul Scholes made it a **2-0** win. But against **Romania**, Viorel Moldovan gave England's opponents the lead. Glenn Hoddle called for **Michael Owen** to come on, and within minutes the 18-year-old grabbed an **equaliser**, then hit the post in the closing moments. But in between Chelsea's **Dan Petrescu** had grabbed the **winner**. It was another **2-0** win against **Colombia**, though, with a fine goal from **Darren Anderton** and a superb **David Beckham** free kick.

ouch!

HOW THEY FINISHED

ENGLAND'S POSITION AFTER ALL THREE
WORLD CUP GROUP G GAMES

	P	W	D	L	F	A	Pts
Romania	3	2	1	0	4	2	7
England	**3**	**2**	**0**	**1**	**5**	**2**	**6**
Colombia	3	1	0	2	1	3	3
Tunisia	3	0	1	2	1	4	1

MATCH STATS

Sheeeea-rer!

England 2 Tunisia 0

Shearer 42, Scholes 90

DATE	15 June 1998	**VENUE**	Marseille
H/T	1-0	**ATT**	54,587

David Seaman
Gareth Southgate
Tony Adams
Sol Campbell
Graeme Le Saux
Paul Ince
David Batty
Darren Anderton
Paul Scholes
Teddy Sheringham (Michael Owen, 84)
Alan Shearer

England 1 Romania 2

Owen 83   Moldovan 47, Petrescu 90

DATE	22 June 1998	**VENUE**	Toulouse
H/T	0-0	**ATT**	37,500

David Seaman
Gary Neville
Tony Adams
Sol Campbell
Graeme Le Saux
Paul Ince (David Beckham, 33)
David Batty
Darren Anderton
Paul Scholes
Teddy Sheringham (Michael Owen, 73)
Alan Shearer

England 2 Colombia 0

Anderton 20, Beckham 30

DATE	26 June 1998	**VENUE**	Lens
H/T	2-0	**ATT**	41,275

David Seaman
Gary Neville
Tony Adams
Sol Campbell
Graeme Le Saux
Paul Ince (David Batty, 82)
Darren Anderton (Rob Lee, 79)
David Beckham
Paul Scholes (Steve McManaman, 73)
Michael Owen
Alan Shearer

" There's only
one team
that's going to win it now
and that's
England"

TV pundit *KEVIN KEEGAN* **puts his foot in his mouth
after Michael Owen's equaliser against Romania**

If Only...

An **unbelievable match**, full of **heartbreak**, **magic**, and awful **mistakes**. After David Seaman conceded an early penalty, **Michael Owen** won one back. He then scored a **wonderful goal**, running from the halfway line to smash the ball home. But a smart free kick move made it **2-2** on the stroke of half time. Then **David Beckham** was sent off for **retaliating**. England's **ten players** fought heroically, and **Sol Campbell** even had a goal **disallowed**. The referee ignored a good handball appeal in extra time, too. It came down to **penalties**. **Paul Ince** and **David Batty** missed, and England were out.

DID YOU KNOW?

This was the **second year** running Michael Owen had been knocked out of the World Championships by **Argentina** – in 1997 he was in the England team that lost 2-1 in the last 16 of the **World Under-20 tournament**, held in Malaysia.

ARGENTINA

FRANCE '98 ROUND 2

Owen scores the goal of the tournament

Beckham sees red

> The players gave **eveything** The whole country can be very **proud**

GLENN HODDLE reflects on the dramatic game with Argentina

Batty misses. Doh!

England **2**
Shearer 10 (pen), Owen 16

Argentina **2**
Batistuta 6 (pen), Zanetti 45

ARGENTINA WIN 4-3 ON PENALTIES

DATE 30 June 1998   **VENUE** Saint-Etienne
H/T   2-2

ENGLAND

David Seaman ▪
Gary Neville
Tony Adams
Sol Campbell
Darren Anderton (David Batty, 96)
David Beckham ▮
Paul Ince ▪
Graeme Le Saux ▪ (G Southgate, 70)
Paul Scholes (Paul Merson 78)
Michael Owen
Alan Shearer

ARGENTINA

Carlos Roa ▪
Nelson Vivas
Roberto Ayala
Jose Chamot
Javier Zanetti
Matias Almeyda ▪
Diego Simeone ▪ (Berti, 91)
Ariel Ortega
Juan Veron ▪
Gabriel Batistuta (Crespo, 68)
Claudio Lopez (Gallardo, 68)

PENALTY SHOOT-OUT

Berti	Scored	**Shearer**	Scored
Crespo	Saved	**Ince**	Saved
Veron	Scored	**Merson**	Scored
Gallardo	Scored	**Owen**	Scored
Ayala	Scored	**Batty**	Saved

Fast Starters

The Euro 2000 Qualifying campaign got off to **a great start** in Stockholm, with **Alan Shearer** putting England ahead within two minutes – but it was all downhill from there. In the absence of the suspended David Beckham it was the captain who smashed the ball home from a free kick after **76 seconds**. But **Sweden equalised** when David Seaman couldn't hold a free kick, letting in **Andersson**, and went ahead when defensive confusion allowed **Mjallby** to make it 2-1. Things got still worse when **Paul Ince** was **sent off** in the second half, and there was no way back.

Scholes plays his heart out

Lee replaces Anderton

HOW THEY STAND

ENGLAND'S POSITION AFTER THIS MATCH

	P	W	D	L	F	A	Pts
Poland	1	1	0	0	3	0	3
Sweden	1	1	0	0	2	1	3
England	**1**	**0**	**0**	**1**	**1**	**2**	**0**
Bulgaria	1	0	0	1	0	3	0
Luxembourg	0	0	0	0	0	0	0

"If there is a consolation it's better having a defeat now rather than near the end of the qualifying group"

DAVID SEAMAN stays optimistic

SWEDEN

MATCH STATS

DATE
5 September 1998

VENUE
Solna, Sweden

eyeing up the Swedish goal

Sweden   2
Andersson 30, Mjallby 32

England   1
Shearer 2

HALF-TIME SCORE	ATTENDANCE
2-1	35,000

ENGLAND
David Seaman
Sol Campbell (Paul Merson, 75)
Graeme Le Saux
Tony Adams
Gareth Southgate
Paul Ince ▮
Darren Anderton (Rob Lee, 43)
Jamie Redknapp ▮
Paul Scholes (Teddy Sheringham, 87)
Michael Owen ▮
Alan Shearer

SWEDEN
Magnus Hedman
Roland Nilsson
Patrik Andersson
Joachim Bjorklund
Pontus Kamark (Teddy Lucic, 83)
Stefan Schwarz ▮
Andreas Andersson (D Andersson, 90)
Johan Mjallby
Fredrik Ljungberg
Henrik Larsson
Jorgen Pettersson

Pressing For Victory

Bulgaria came to Wembley after a **3-0 home defeat** by Poland. They had lost their last match of France 98 **6-1 to Spain**. So even after the defeat in Sweden, there were plenty of **grounds for optimism**. But the row caused by **Glenn Hoddle's World Cup Diary** rumbled on, and the team seemed far from happy. **Michael Owen** had a reasonable chance early on, but it turned into another disappointing afternoon. **Jamie Redknapp**, given the creative role, was also disappointing, and in truth it was a **poor performance** all round.

BULGARIA

EURO 2000 QUALIFIER

blocked again!

MATCH STATS

DATE
10 October 1998
VENUE
Wembley

England	**0**
Bulgaria	**0**

HALF-TIME SCORE
0-0

ATTENDANCE
72,974

ENGLAND

David Seaman
Gary Neville
Andy Hinchcliffe (G Le Saux, 35)
Sol Campbell
Gareth Southgate
Rob Lee
Darren Anderton ▪ (David Batty, 67)
Jamie Redknapp ▪
Paul Scholes (Teddy Sheringham, 76)
Michael Owen
Alan Shearer

BULGARIA

Zdravko Zdravkov
Radostin Kichichev ▪
Zlatomir Zagorchich
Valentin Ivanov
Ivailo Yordanov
Zlatko Iankov
Rossen Kirilov
Hristo Stoichkov (Gheorghi Bachev, 60)
Marian Hristov (Gheorghi Ivanov, 90)
Milen Petkov
Ilian Iliev (Ilia Gruev, 63)

HOW THEY STAND

Le Saux gives his all

ENGLAND'S POSITION AFTER THIS MATCH

	P	W	D	L	F	A	Pts
Poland	2	2	0	0	6	0	6
Sweden	1	1	0	0	2	1	3
England	**2**	**0**	**1**	**1**	**1**	**2**	**1**
Bulgaria	2	0	1	1	0	3	1
Luxembourg	1	0	0	1	0	3	0

"We mustn't get carried away that it's all **doom** and **gloom**"

GLENN HODDLE after the disappointing display against Bulgaria

Back To Winning Ways

Four days after drawing with Bulgaria, **England at last won** a Euro 2000 qualifying game. Before England took the lead, though, **Dan Theis** missed a fifth minute penalty, **blazing over** after David Seaman had felled Marcel Christophe trying to reach a **poor header** from **Gareth Southgate**. But **Michael Owen** then scored with a neat turn and shot, **Alan Shearer** doubled Theis' penalty misery when the Luxembourger handled. The second half was then a let-down, with just **Southgate's late goal**. Still, a win was what was needed.

Congrats for Owen

Ian Wright, Wright, Wright…

HOW THEY STAND

ENGLAND'S POSITION AFTER THIS MATCH

	P	W	D	L	F	A	Pts
Poland	2	2	0	0	6	0	6
Sweden	2	2	0	0	3	1	6
England	**3**	**1**	**1**	**1**	**4**	**2**	**4**
Bulgaria	3	0	1	2	0	4	1
Luxembourg	2	0	0	2	0	6	0

LUXEMBOURG

Anderton goes close

MATCH STATS

DATE
14 October 1998

VENUE
Luxembourg

Luxembourg 0
England 3

Owen 18, Shearer 38 (pen), Southgate 88

HALF-TIME SCORE
0-2

ATTENDANCE
8,000

ENGLAND

David Seaman
Rio Ferdinand
Phil Neville
Sol Campbell
Gareth Southgate
David Batty
David Beckham
Darren Anderton (Rob Lee, 64)
Paul Scholes (Ian Wright, 77)
Alan Shearer
Michael Owen

LUXEMBOURG

Paul Koch
Ralph Ferron
Nicolas Funck
Laurent Deville
Jeff Strasser
Jeff Saibene
Daniel Theis (Luc Holtz, 61)
Frank Deville (Christian Alverdi, 85)
Marcel Christophe (Paolo Amodio, 78)
Manuel Cardoni
Patrick Posing

Becks nips one in

"There are no cricket scores any more in world football"

GLENN HODDLE **after England have to settle for just the three goals**

Lions Roar

Had England lost this game, no-one would have been surprised if this had been **Glenn Hoddle's last game** in charge. In the opening 20 minutes it threatened to be a bad night against a **fine Czech side** who would later become the **first team to qualify** for Euro 2000 by winning their first seven games. But then **Darren Anderton** scored a neat goal, squeezing the ball in after Ian Wright crossed, then **Paul Merson** combined with Wright and Dion Dublin to make it 2-0. In the second half, **David Beckham** ran the game, and **Rio Ferdinand** brought the ball forward brilliantly. Aston Villa's **Lee Hendrie** almost scored on his debut.

DID YOU KNOW?

The **Czech Republic's previous appearance** at Wembley was the **final of Euro 96**, when they lost **2-1 to Germany**. Had England not lost on penalties in the semi-final, then that final would have been against **Terry Venables' side**.

...Mers's one-two-three...

...heading for the line...

...goal!

CZECH REPUBLIC

a great night for Rio

"**Rio**
has that ability to come out with the ball when the time is **right**"

MARTIN KEOWN on the rampaging Rio Ferdinand

MATCH STATS

DATE
18 November 1998
VENUE
Wembley

England	**2**

Anderton 22, Merson 39

Czech Rep	**0**

HALF-TIME SCORE
2-0

ATTENDANCE
38,535

ENGLAND

Nigel Martyn
Sol Campbell
Martin Keown
Rio Ferdinand
Graeme Le Saux
Nicky Butt
David Beckham
Darren Anderton
Dion Dublin
Ian Wright (Robbie Fowler, 70)
Paul Merson (Lee Hendrie, 76)

CZECH REPUBLIC

Petr Kouba
Radoslav Latal (Miroslav Baranek, 46)
Tomas Votava
Jiri Novotny (Vratislav Lokvenc, 46)
Tomas Repka
Patrik Berger
Jiri Nemec (Roman Vonasek, 46)
Karel Poborsky
Pavel Kuka (Radek Sloncik, 73)
Vladimir Smicer (Martin Kotulek, 46)
Radek Bejbl

French Fried

Glenn Hoddle's departure as coach after a controversial interview happened just before **World Champions France** came to Wembley, so **Howard Wilkinson** took charge, with a squad already selected by Hoddle. **Lee Dixon** was recalled for his first game since 1993, though, after injuries struck. The game started brightly for England, **Michael Owen** being denied an early goal when his shot hit **Fabien Barthez's body**. But as the match wore on **Zinedine Zidane** started to control the midfield, and Arsenal's **Nicolas Anelka** scored twice and had another wrongly disallowed for offside. England ran out of ideas.

DID YOU KNOW?

Howard Wilkinson became England's **third caretaker** manager or coach, after **Joe Mercer** in 1974, and **Ron Greenwood** in 1977. Greenwood then became full-time manager until the 1982 World Cup finals.

FRANCE

INTERNATIONAL FRIENDLY

Spice Boy flies against the French

Owen makes it his

Anelka makes life hard for England

MATCH STATS

DATE
10 February 1999

VENUE
Wembley

England	0
France	**2**

Anelka 69, 76

HALF-TIME SCORE
0-0

ATTENDANCE
74,111

ENGLAND

David Seaman (Nigel Martyn, 46)
Lee Dixon (Rio Ferdinand, 72)
Graeme Le Saux
Tony Adams
Martin Keown (Jason Wilcox, 85)
Paul Ince
David Beckham
Jamie Redknapp (Paul Scholes, 85)
Darren Anderton
Alan Shearer
Michael Owen (Andy Cole, 66)

FRANCE

Fabien Barthez
Lilian Thuram
Laurent Blanc (Frank Leboeuf, 46)
Marcel Desailly
Bixente Lizarazu
Didier Deschamps (Vincent Candela, 90)
Emmanuel Petit
Zinedine Zidane
Youri Djorkaeff (Patrick Vieira, 83)
Robert Pires (Christophe Dugarry, 46)
Nicolas Anelka (Sylvain Wiltord, 83)

> " **When I told my kids I was in the England team they burst out** crying "

LEE DIXON (his kids thought playing for England meant he was leaving Arsenal)

Magnificent!

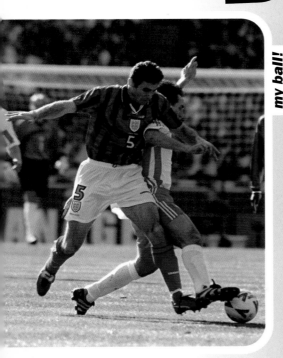

my ball!

England had **another new coach** to face Poland in a game England had to win – and **Kevin Keegan** delivered the **three points**, thanks to **three goals** from **Paul Scholes**. The first came when he flicked the ball over the keeper after 11 minutes. It was **2-0** with 21 minutes gone when **David Beckham's cross** was turned in, though the ball did seem to hit Scholes' hand. Poland came back into it after **Jerzy Brzeczek** lost his marker – Scholes – to score. But the **Manchester United star** got his **hat trick** with a header on Alan Shearer's flick.

POLAND

EURO 2000 QUALIFIER

MATCH STATS

DATE
27 March 1999

VENUE
Wembley

England   3
Scholes 11, 21, 70

Poland   1
Brzeczek 29

HALF-TIME SCORE   **ATTENDANCE**
0-0   73,836

ENGLAND
David Seaman
Gary Neville
Graeme Le Saux
Martin Keown
Sol Campbell
Tim Sherwood
David Beckham (Phil Neville, 78)
Paul Scholes (Jamie Redknapp, 82)
Steve McManaman (Ray Parlour, 69)
Alan Shearer
Andy Cole

POLAND
Adam Matysek
Jacek Bak
Tomasz Lapinski
Krzysztof Ratajczyk
Jacek Zielinski
Tomasz Hajto
Poitr Swierczewski (Tomasz Klos, 46)
Tomasz Iwan
Rafal Siadaczka (Wojciech Kowalczyk, 64)
Jerzy Brzeczek
Miroslaw Trzeciak (Andrzej Juskowiak, 82)

ginger spice!

HOW THEY STAND

ENGLAND'S POSITION AFTER THIS MATCH

	P	W	D	L	F	A	Pts
Sweden	3	3	0	0	5	1	9
England	**4**	**2**	**1**	**1**	**7**	**3**	**7**
Poland	3	2	0	1	7	3	6
Bulgaria	3	0	1	2	0	4	1
Luxembourg	3	0	0	3	0	8	0

" The match ball is going **straight** on the mantlepiece **"**

A delighted *PAUL SCHOLES* after his hat trick

Full-Time Commitme

England went to Budapest for a friendly for **Kevin Keegan's second match** of his four games in charge as caretaker – but very quickly afterwards he stated that he wanted the job **full time**, and soon a deal was done with **Fulham**. The big point of the game in Hungary was **a chance to experiment**, and Manchester United's **Wes Brown** and Sunderland's **Kevin Phillips** were in the starting line-up. Three more players made their debuts as substitutes: Phillips' colleague **Michael Gray**, Liverpool's **Jamie Carragher**, and Leicester's **Emile Heskey**. The goals came from a penalty, then a late free kick.

Rio keeps it tight

DID YOU KNOW?

Hungary inflicted **England's record defeat** – in the same stadium as this game. They won **7-1 in 1954**, after they had won **6-3 at Wembley** in 1953, the largest defeat there by a non-British country.

" It was a **treme**
night and I hope I showe
and that h

HUNGARY

INTERNATIONAL FRIENDLY

MATCH STATS

DATE
28 April 1999

VENUE
Budapest

Hungary 1
Hrutka 76

England 1
Shearer 21 (pen)

HALF-TIME SCORE	ATTENDANCE
0-1	45,000

ENGLAND
David Seaman
Wes Brown (Michael Gray, 74)
Phil Neville
Rio Ferdinand (Jamie Carragher, 62)
Martin Keown
David Batty
Nicky Butt
Tim Sherwood
Steve McManaman (Redknapp, 85)
Alan Shearer
Kevin Phillips (Emile Heskey, 83)

OPPONENTS
Gabor Kiraly
Janos Hrutka
Gyorgy Korsos (Norbert Toth, 65)
Janos Matyus
Vilmos Sebok
Gabor Halmai
Tibor Dombi
Pal Dardai
Istvan Pisont (Joszef Somogyi, 46)
Bela Illes
Attila Kosos

On a night for new faces, Keown added much-needed experience

...ndous

...evin Keegan something

...ill keep me in future squads "

KEVIN PHILLIPS after his international debut

Settle For A Draw

After his joy at Wembley against Poland, **Paul Scholes** had a terrible day against Sweden, when he became the first England player to be **sent off** at home, for two bookable offences. That, and an **injury to David Beckham** that saw him forced to limp off, left England **grateful for a point** from a game they had gone out to win. Without the injured Michael Owen, **Andy Cole** was up front with **Alan Shearer**, but they **didn't get a shot** at goal between them. A difficult day all round, and with **ten men for the last 40 minutes** a draw was a relief.

Cole's not happy...

HOW THEY STAND

ENGLAND'S POSITION AFTER THIS MATCH

	P	W	D	L	F	A	Pts
Sweden	5	4	1	0	6	1	13
Poland	5	3	0	2	9	4	9
England	**5**	**2**	**2**	**1**	**7**	**3**	**8**
Bulgaria	5	1	1	3	2	6	4
Luxembourg	4	0	0	4	0	10	0

SWEDEN

Neville gets it over

Gray makes his mark

MATCH STATS

DATE
5 June 1999

VENUE
Wembley

England 0

Sweden 0

HALF-TIME SCORE
0-0

ATTENDANCE
75,824

ENGLAND
David Seaman
Phil Neville
Graeme Le Saux (Michael Gray, 46)
Martin Keown (Ferdinand, 34)
Sol Campbell
Tim Sherwood
David Batty
David Beckham (Ray Parlour, 76)
Paul Scholes
Andy Cole
Alan Shearer

SWEDEN
Magnus Hedman
Roland Nilsson
Patrik Andersson
Joachim Bjorklund
Pontus Kamark
Stefan Schwarz
Hakan Mild (Niclas Alexandersson, 7)
Johan Mjallby (D Andersson, 82)
Fredrik Ljungberg
Henrik Larsson (Magnus Svensson, 69)
Kennet Andersson

"This feels like a **victory** I didn't have **anything** to do"

Sweden's goalkeeper *MAGNUS HEDMAN* on his side's domination

Chasing The Dream

A **win** in Sofia would have done a lot to **lift England**. It seemed a good possibility when **Alan Shearer scored** after 15 minutes, turning sharply to hit a shot across the keeper into his right hand corner. But the **lead only lasted three minutes**, after a free kick was swung in and **headed home by Markov** at the far post. In the second half England were up against **ten men**, but couldn't recapture the lead. Kevin Keegan's side were left having to **win their last two games** to reach the Euro 2000 play-offs, home to Luxembourg then away to Poland.

Seaman – rock at the back

Owen sets off on a run

HOW THEY STAND

ENGLAND'S POSITION AFTER THIS MATCH

	P	W	D	L	F	A	Pts
Sweden	5	4	1	0	6	1	13
Poland	6	4	0	2	12	6	12
England	**6**	**2**	**3**	**1**	**8**	**4**	**9**
Bulgaria	6	1	2	3	3	7	5
Luxembourg	5	0	0	5	2	13	0

BULGARIA

Keegan battles om

MATCH STATS

DATE
9 June 1999
VENUE
Sofia

Bulgaria 1
Markov 18

England 1
Shearer 15

HALF-TIME SCORE
1-1

ATTENDANCE
22,000

ENGLAND

David Seaman
Phil Neville
Michael Gray
Jonathan Woodgate (Parlour, 63)
Gareth Southgate
Sol Campbell
David Batty
Jamie Redknapp
Teddy Sheringham
Alan Shearer
Robbie Fowler (Emile Heskey, 80)

BULGARIA

Dimitar Ivankov
Radostin Kichichev
Zlatomir Zagorchich
Stanimir Stoilov
Gheorghi Markov
Rossen Kirilov
Stiliyan Petrov
Hristo Stoichkov (Gheorghi Bachev, 72)
Hristo Yovov (Martin Petrov, 46)
Milen Petkov
Ilian Iliev (Daniel Borimirov, 60)

"
The lads have given it their
best shot
but that just has not been good enough
"

A downcast *KEVIN KEEGAN* after another draw

David Beckham

After getting **sent off** against Argentina, David Beckham's stock could not have been lower. But how **England missed him** during his suspension! He came back in against Luxembourg, and soon he was the **best player** against the **Czechs**, the **French** and above all the **Poles**. The agony of watching him leave the pitch **injured against Sweden** in June was a **sad end** to a year when he reached the heights with his club and showed for his country the **great talent** that promises so much for the future.

Take that! Another Beckham free-kick special

YOUNG PLAYER OF THE YEAR

Rio Ferdinand

The **West Ham** defender had a good year for his country, recovering from the **disappointment** of being omitted from **France 98**. Though sometimes he **played himself into trouble**, a generally sound defender and one of the few England players **willing to run at the opposition** with the ball.

All the highs...

Best Game

The **3-1 win over Poland** rekindled belief in England, with **Kevin Keegan's reign** getting off to the perfect start thanks to **Paul Scholes' hat trick**.

Best Individual Performance

Michael Owen was outstanding against **Argentina**. He won the **penalty** to get England back in the game, scored a **fabulous goal**, and then converted his **shootout kick**.

Best Comeback

To go a goal behind against **Argentina** so early on could have finished many teams, but England at that point were **made of sterner stuff**, came back, led, and **should have won**. Alas.

Best Moment

David Beckham dinked the ball forward to **Michael Owen** in the centre circle, who played it into his stride then **ran and ran and ran** before **blasting** the ball past Carlos Roa for an **amazing goal**.

WORST

Worst Game

A lot of contenders, but the way that **France dominated England at Wembley** put the team to shame. The loss of Glenn Hoddle didn't help, but this was a **poor show** against the World Champions.

Worst Individual Performance

Steve McManaman might have been playing on the wrong wing **against Poland**, but was **very poor** while all his **teammates were inspired** by Kevin Keegan.

Worst Collapse

To lead **Sweden** after just 76 seconds was a dream start, but the way **England surrendered that lead** so lamely showed how much the **spirit had gone** after France 98.

Worst Moment

Quite a few to choose from, but **David Batty's penalty** against Argentina that **lost the shootout** stands out equally with the moment in the same game when **David Beckham** got his marching orders.

QUIZ

1 Who was the **first player** to make his **England debut** this season?

2 How many **away games** did England win this year (**not counting World Cup** games in neutral France)?

3 **Which player** has been distorted by our artist in the picture to the right?

4 Who scored **a hat trick** for England?

5 How many **different coaches** led England out?

6 **How many** England players were **sent off** in the year from June 1998 to June 1999?

7 Which team **missed a penalty** in normal play against England?

8 With which **team** did England **draw twice**?

9 Which **club** had **two England debutants** in the same match and who were the opponents?

10 Who was **England's last caretaker manager** before Howard Wilkinson?

Answers

1 Lee Hendrie **2** One **3** Darren Anderton **4** Paul Scholes **5** Three **6** Three **7** Luxembourg **8** Bulgaria **9** Sunderland, against Hungary **10** Ron Greenwood